Why Would Elephants Rather Play Tag?

Por qué los elefantes prefieren jugar a la mancha by Silvina Rocha and illustrated by mEy!
Original edition ©2013 by Pequeño Editor, Buenos Aires, Argentina
www.pequenoeditor.com

Text copyright © 2013 by Silvina Rocha
Illustrations copyright © 2013 by mEy!
English translation copyright © 2015 by Doubledutch Books
First published in English in Canada and the USA in 2015 by Doubledutch Books

Printed in Canada by Friesens

Library and Archives Canada Cataloguing in Publication

Rocha, Silvina, 1969-
[Por qué los elefantes prefieren jugar a la mancha. English]
    Why would elephants rather play tag? / Silvina Rocha ; illustrator, mEy!
; translator, Silvana Goldemberg.

Translation of: Por qué los elefantes prefieren jugar a la mancha.
ISBN 978-0-9940570-6-8 (paperback)

    I. mEy!, 1985-, illustrator II. Goldemberg, Silvana, 1963-, translator
III. Title. IV. Title: Por qué los elefantes prefieren jugar a la mancha. English.

PZ7.R62359Wh 2015   j863'.7   C2015-905289-0

www.doubledutchbooks.com
www.facebook.com/doubledutchbooks

Doubledutch Books
1427 Somerville Ave.,
Winnipeg, MB
Canada R3T 1C3

SILVINA ROCHA · MEY!

TRANSLATED BY SILVANA GOLDEMBERG

Why Would Elephants Rather Play Tag?

doubledutch
books

Elephant, Cat, Mouse, and Bee
decide to play hide and seek.

Mouse closes his eyes and
starts to count out loud.

1 2 3 4 5

The others race away
to find a place to hide.

Bee chooses a
matchbox.

Can a bee fit inside a matchbox?

Cat climbs into
the piano.

Can a cat fit inside a piano?

Elephant thinks, and thinks,
and thinks, and thinks.

Can an elephant fit inside
a wardrobe?

I SEE YOU, ELEPHANT

YOU'RE IT!

Elephant closes his eyes and starts to count out loud.

The others race away to find
a place to hide.

7

6

5

4

3

Mouse jumps into
a kitchen drawer.

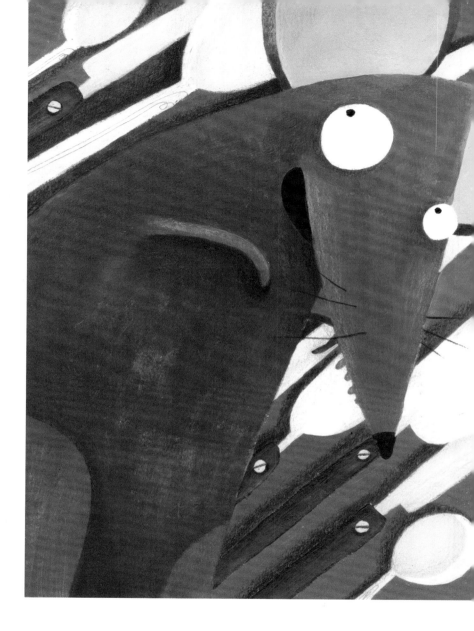

Can a mouse fit inside a kitchen drawer?

Bee hides behind
the petals of a daisy.

Can a bee fit behind the petals of a daisy?

Cat leaps into a bucket.

Oh, no! The bucket is full of water.

Cat quickly jumps onto the clothes in a laundry basket.

Elephant finishes counting
just as Bee peeks around...

I SEE YOU, BEE! YOU'R

20

Now, Bee closes her eyes and starts to count in her buzzing bee voice.

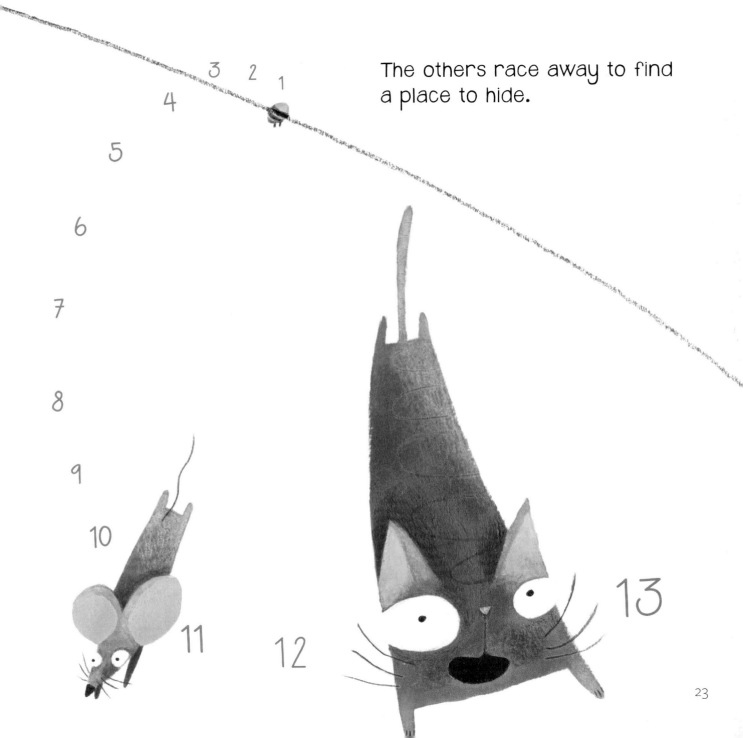

The others race away to find a place to hide.

Mouse scurries into
Cat's mouth.

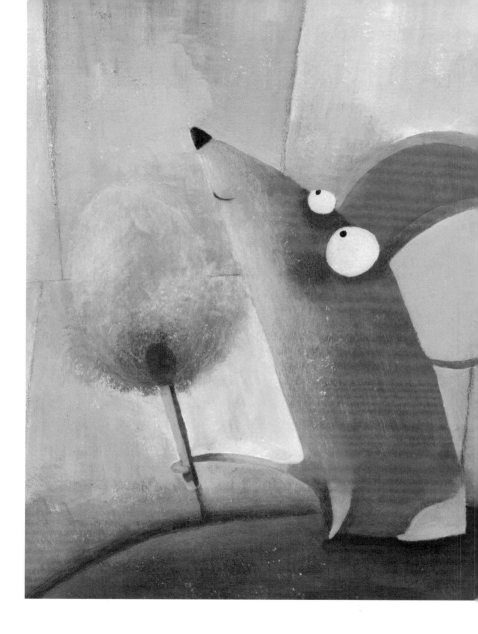

Can a mouse fit inside a cat's mouth?

Cat crawls inside a rolled-up carpet.

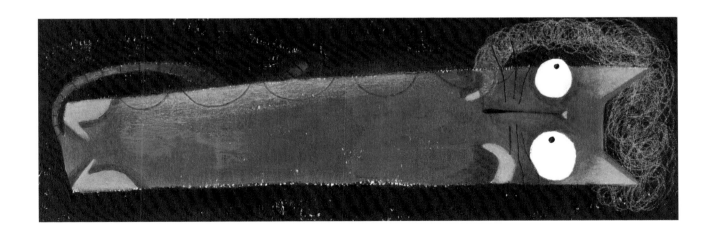

Can a cat fit inside a rolled-up carpet?

But where can Elephant hide?
He thinks, and thinks, and thinks...

under a table?

Can an elephant fit
inside a car?

behind a bookshelf?

inside an oven?

behind the window curtains?

under a desk?

inside a refrigerator?

NO, N

AND NO!

NO

No matter how hard Elephant tries,
he can't find a place to hide.

That's why